The Littlest Family's Big Day

Emily Winfield Martin

Random House New York

One morning, very early,
a little family came to the woods.

They found a place
just big enough for all
their little things.

Then they set out on a wander
to see what they would find.

Were they alone?

. . . to wander on the water.

Up along the riverbank,
they found a place to rest.

But—oh no!—they couldn't rest for long . . .

. . . because they had to run!

They ran
and ran
and the rain pelted down until . . .

When the rain stopped,
the little family found
that they were Lost.

But when you are Lost,
it is the best time to be Found.

When their wander was done—
after hello and goodbye,
and the breeze and the wind,
and the river and the wild,
and the rain and the warm,
and after Lost—

they found they were . . .

Good night, little wanderers!

To my own
Mr. Bear

Copyright © 2016 by Emily Winfield Martin

All rights reserved. Published in the United States by Random House Children's Books,
a division of Penguin Random House LLC, New York.

Random House and the colophon are registered trademarks of Penguin Random House LLC.

Visit us on the Web! randomhousekids.com

Educators and librarians, for a variety of teaching tools, visit us at RHTeachersLibrarians.com

Library of Congress Cataloging-in-Publication Data
Name: Martin, Emily Winfield, author, illustrator.
Title: The Littlest Family's big day / by Emily Winfield Martin.
Description: First edition. | New York : Random House, [2016] | Summary: "The Littlest Family goes wandering in the woods
and just when they think they are lost, they find their way home again." —Provided by publisher.
Identifiers: LCCN 2015030980 | ISBN 978-0-553-51101-7 (hardcover) |
ISBN 978-0-375-97431-1 (lib. bdg.) | ISBN 978-0-553-51102-4 (ebook)
Subjects: | CYAC: Family life—Fiction. | Size—Fiction.
Classification: LCC PZ7.M356833 Li 2016 | DDC [E]—dc23
LC record available at http://lccn.loc.gov/2015030980

The illustrations for this book were created using acrylic on wood and gouache on hot pressed watercolor paper.

Book design by Nicole de las Heras

MANUFACTURED IN CHINA
10 9 8 7 6 5 4 3 2 1
First Edition